For Nancy—for making this happen!
—R.H.H.

To Robie, who had to put up with a lot
—N.H.

The illustrator wishes to acknowledge
Evan Sult, her production consultant.

Text copyright © 2005 by Bee Productions, Inc.
Illustrations copyright © 2005 by Nicole Hollander

Little, Brown and Company

Time Warner Book Group
1271 Avenue of the Americas, New York, NY 10020
Visit our Web site at www.lb-kids.com

First Edition

Library of Congress Cataloging-in-Publication Data
Harris, Robie H.
  I'm not sleepy! / by Robie Harris ; illustrated by Nicole Hollander.—1st ed.
    p. cm.—(Just being me)
  Summary: A little boy claims not to be sleepy, but after his father falls asleep in his bed while reading a story, the boy, his cat, and his parents are all ready for bedtime. Includes brief notes on helping a child go to sleep.
  ISBN 0-316-10941-X
  [1. Bedtime—Fiction. 2. Parent and child—Fiction.] I. Title: I am not sleepy!. II. Hollander, Nicole, ill. III. Title.
PZ7.H2436Iabe 2005
[E]—dc22
                                                                                                    2004013941

10 9 8 7 6 5 4 3 2 1

IM

Printed in China

The illustrations for this book were done in pen and ink. Color was added using Adobe Photoshop.
The text was set in Providence and Sylvia (designed by Nicole Hollander and Tom Greensfelder),
and the display type is Drunk Cyrillic.

I'm NOT Sleepy!

By Robie H. Harris

Illustrated by Nicole Hollander

LITTLE, BROWN AND COMPANY

New York ⁓ Boston

"It's bedtime!" said Mommy.
"No bedtime!" I said. "No sleep time!
I'm still playing with Kitty."

Kitty leaped onto my bed.
I tickled her tummy and she curled up into a big ball.

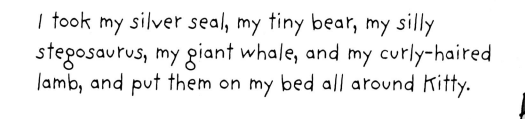

I took my silver seal, my tiny bear, my silly stegosaurus, my giant whale, and my curly-haired lamb, and put them on my bed all around Kitty.

"There's still some room for you," said Daddy.

"It's story time," I said. "NOT bedtime!"
"Okay," said Daddy.
"But after your story, it's bedtime."

Daddy read my CRAZY CAT book to me.
"Sleepy?" he asked when he finished.
"No-oooooo!" I sang.

Then daddy yawned a big yawn.
"Read it to me one more time?" I asked.

"The crazy cat...," Daddy began, "jumped onto...
the magician's...head...and the...and the..."

Daddy yawned again. His eyes closed.
The book slipped out of his hands.
Daddy was asleep!

DAddy,
YOUR eyes
ARe CLoseD!

Daddy snored. I giggled.
He snored louder. I giggled louder.

I pulled my big red blanket over Daddy
and put my giant whale next to his cheek.
I gave him a kiss and whispered,
"Good night! Sleep tight!"

Then I showed my animals the pictures in my book.
Soon, I was a little sleepy.

ZZZZZ...

ZZZZZ...

When Mommy came in to say good night, she looked at Daddy and giggled.

"It's NOT funny!" I said.
"I want to go to bed now.
But I can't! Daddy's on my bed!"

"Let's wake him up!" said Mommy.
"Let's tickle him!" I said.
"Wake up, Daddy —
so I can go to bed!"

Daddy opened his eyes and laughed the biggest, loudest laugh. Kitty sat up and screeched.

"Okay," he said. And I climbed back onto my bed.
Daddy and Mommy tucked me in tight.

I snuggled under my covers with my giant whale.
Daddy yawned. Mommy yawned.
Then I yawned too.

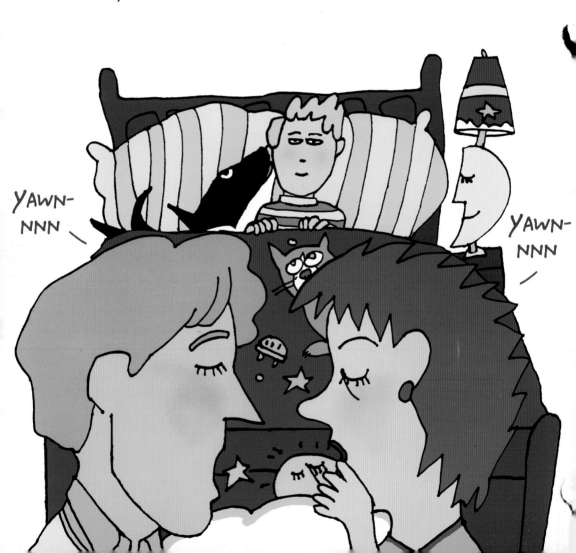

And they turned out the light.
Kitty curled up into a big ball—and purred.

"Good night, sleepy Kitty!" I whispered.
Soon, Kitty fell asleep. And soon, I fell asleep too.

What's Going On?

For young children, going to bed is not always easy and can take a long time—which can be tiring for any parent. It isn't just that young children may have more energy than their parents at the end of the day. Going to sleep can also be scary for a young child because it means leaving a parent behind, even if just for the night. Children worry about who will chase away bad dreams, who will keep them safe through the night, and who will be there when they wake up.

Bedtime rituals bring comfort to the uncertainties of falling asleep: making the bed feel just right with a favorite pillow, having a cuddle and a story, being sure a light is on to chase the night shadows away, and saying "good night" to everyone and everything in the room. The child in this story fills his bed with his stuffed animals, so he can delay bedtime just a little longer. But then his father falls asleep before he does. With his mother's help, the boy wakes his father, and everything is back in order, making it possible to return to his familiar nighttime routine.